THE BEST BOOK
IN THE WORLD!

VISIT SOZI.COM
ORDER FROM
FLYINGEYEBOOKS.COM

SECOND EDITION
PUBLISHED BY
FLYING EYE BOOKS
62 GREAT EASTERN STREET
LONDON EC2A3QR
PRINTED IN BELGIUM
ISBN-10 1909263303
ISBN-13 978-1909263307

The BEST BOOK in the WORLD!

by Rilla

FLYING EYE BOOKS

Take the first step.

Turn the first page.

Read along. Read out loud.

Or in your head.

Follow the story.

Up
Under

Over here.

Where will it take you next?

Across wide open pages.

Through pictures and words.

Page by page you're carried away.

So let yourself go!

And don't be afraid.

We've people to meet...

And worlds to discover.

Enjoy the ride!

We're not heading home.
At least not until we
reach the back cover!

What now? Where next?

Slow down!

Rest your eyes.

We're almost at the end.

Shhh, here's a secret,
the story won't stop...

The BEST BOOK in the WORLD!
by Rilla
FLYING EYE BOOKS

If we go back to the beginning again!